UNCLE'S NEW SUIT

(a sort of true story)

UNCLE'S NEW SUIT

(a sort of true story)

Written and illustrated by Lisa Passen

Henry Holt and Company

New York

Published by Henry Holt and Company, Inc.,
115 West 18th Street, New York, New York 10011.
Published simultaneously in Canada by Fitzhenry & Whiteside Ltd.,
195 Allstate Parkway, Markham, Ontario L3R 4T8.

Library of Congress Cataloging-in-Publication Data
Passen, Lisa.
Uncle's new suit: (a sort of true story) / written and illustrated by Lisa Passen.
Summary: When Uncle Carmen gets a new job, a close-knit Italian
family celebrates by taking him shopping for a new suit.
ISBN 0-8050-1652-X (alk. paper)
[1. Family—Fiction. 2. Italian Americans—Fiction.
3. Shopping—Fiction.] I. Title.
PZ7.P26937Un 1992
[E]—dc20   91-27727

Henry Holt books are available at special discounts
for bulk purchases for sales promotions, premiums,
fund-raising, or educational use. Special editions
or book excerpts can also be created to specification.

Printed in the United States of America
on acid-free paper. ∞

1 3 5 7 9 10 8 6 4 2

For Dad, my favorite artist

Once upon a time, a long, long time ago, back when there was only black-and-white television with just three channels, I was a little girl.

We all lived together in a very old gray-and-green Victorian farmhouse on the busy main street of our town. All of the neighborhood children thought it was a haunted house. It was just a little run-down and crowded. Oh, it was so crowded.

We had the upstairs, my parents, me, my brother Joe, the cats. My mother was a housewife then; she had yet to begin her career as a telephone operator. She would practice singing opera while doing the dishes. She could sing very loudly.

My father worked as a picture framer during the day, but he was really an artist! Brushes, paints, canvases, sketch paper, all over the place. He was always working on a new still-life painting. His models were the prettiest apples and bananas that Mom could find at the market. The two of them slept on a sofa bed in the living room.

My brother and I shared a bedroom with our two cats, Minnie and Tiger, and one little green turtle who lived on a clear plastic island. Sometimes the turtle would escape from his island, but we would always find him sooner or later.

Downstairs lived everyone else. My grandmother, Nana, was always cooking. What a cook! I loved to dip her fresh bread into her homemade tomato sauce. And my grandfather, Poppa, always eating, with a jug of his homemade wine by his side. They kept their dog, Alexander, out in the yard. Alexander was a mix of many, many very rare pedigrees.

My uncle Angelo was a cop who worked the night shift and who usually slept during the day. His wife, my aunt Mary, came from down South. They had three children then, Terry, Margaret, and Angelo, Jr.—there always seemed to be another one on the way.

My uncle Carmen worked as a waiter. He was not married yet, but he was engaged to my aunt Pat. Aunt Pat was pretty, with blond hair that fell down in a flip over one eye and her rhinestone-studded harlequin glasses. She was a hairdresser.

One Saturday afternoon, I was drawing pictures next to my father as he painted. My brother was outside playing, and my mom was reading one of those magazines that tell you how to make your house beautiful. Suddenly, we heard my nana banging loudly on the radiator pipes from downstairs. This was a signal of alert! Nana shouted up to my mother from a window. "Josephine! Come down! Quick! *Vieni!* Hurry! *Vieni!*"

Uh-oh! I knew something was wrong because Nana was mixing up her English and Italian again.

Mom dropped what she was doing and ran down the stairs. "Oh, no! What's happened? What's wrong?"

I dropped my paper and pencils and followed, Minnie and Tiger running ahead of me. Dad set aside his paint brushes and charged after us.

We all burst into Nana's living room. She was shouting so loudly I didn't know what to expect. Had I done something? Was my turtle in her sugar bowl again?

"What is it?" shouted my mom.

"It's your brother Carmen!" said Nana to my mother. Whew! It wasn't me. What did Uncle Carmen do?

Mom looked like she was going to faint. "What is it? What?" she pleaded.

". . . Your brother Carmen . . ." "What? What?" Mom asked again.

"He gotta new job!"

"Oh, Momma!" said my mother to her mother. "Is that all?"

"Is that ALL? He gotta new job! Inna office! A suit job. He gonna wear a suit. No more he be a waiter!"

Poppa came in from his vegetable garden. Uncle Angelo rolled over on the sofa and yawned. Alexander was barking loudly.

"A fine office job," said Nana, proudly. "He in the shower now. When he come out, he tell you all about it."

"Lordy, Lordy!" said Aunt Mary from the kitchen, a baby in one arm, a pan with fried bologna in the other. Fried bologna sandwiches were my aunt Mary's specialty.

My cousins and my brother ran in from the back door. They had been playing soldiers, and my brother had them tied and captured.

Aunt Pat was next to arrive. "Carmen called and I caught the first bus out! Isn't it wonderful news? A new job like this is a step in the right direction."

Uncle Carmen came out of the bathroom and seemed surprised to see so many people around him. "What are you all looking at?" he asked.

"A man that's gonna go places in this world!" announced Poppa.

"Thatsa right!" added Nana. "No more you hafta be a waiter. You gonna be a big man one day."

I think Uncle Carmen was embarrassed because his face turned red and he looked away. "This is just a small job in a large company. I'll have to work very hard to get anywhere."

"So you'll work hard," said Mom. "My baby brother is a hard worker."

"And you gonna need a new suit! You gotta look good for your first day on the job," said Nana.

"I don't have enough money to buy a new suit right now," said Uncle Carmen as he looked down at the floor.

"Well, we can look, can't we? Come on, *andiamo! Andiamo!* We go take a walk. All of us. We go look at the store window," said Nana.

"I don't know . . ." said Uncle Carmen.

"Oh, Car—it wouldn't hurt to look!" pleaded Aunt Pat as she planted a kiss on Uncle's cheek.

Uncle Carmen didn't have a chance. We all surrounded him, and he received a family escort down the block to Mr. Herbie's for Men and Boys.

When we got there, we found Aunt Flo, Uncle Tom, and Cousin Tommy waiting by the door. Aunt Flo ran over to Uncle Carmen and gave him a big hug. "Momma called and told us. Congratulations on the new job, Car!" gushed Aunt Flo. Uncle Carmen was blushing.

"Look at all these gorgeous suits!" exclaimed Aunt Pat.

"They're all very nice, but . . ." said Uncle Carmen.

"Let's just go in . . ." said Nana, ". . . and get a better look!"

"Maybe another day . . ." replied Uncle Carmen.

"Another day and we might not all be here together. Let's go look today!" said Nana.

How could Uncle say no? My family went in the store, Nana pushing Uncle Carmen and Aunt Pat pulling.

My mother's and Uncle Carmen's cousins Millie and Millie were inside the store, browsing through the handkerchiefs. "Hiya, Carmen. Good luck with your new job! How's this hanky look on ya?" said one of the Millies.

A small man with a small skinny mustache, who was wearing a dark blue suit with a white flower in his lapel, greeted us. "Hello, I'm Mr. Herbie," he said with his nose in the air. "May I be of assistance?"

"We're just looking," Uncle Carmen insisted.

"Just look at this!" said Nana, holding a jet-black blazer up to Uncle Carmen's shoulders.

"I think THIS one is much more elegant," added Aunt Pat.

"What snazzy ties they have in this place!" exclaimed Aunt Flo.

Just then, my other aunt Mary and her three children strolled in the door. This was great. More kids to play with. "Mary!" said Uncle Carmen, surprised.

"Hi, honey! I hear you got a new job! Lots and lots of luck!"

"Carmen," said Nana. "Why don't you just try this suit on? I like to see how it looks on you. Just, just to see."

"Oh, Mama," sighed Uncle Carmen. "I really don't have the money today!"

But the men of the family guided Uncle Carmen to the dressing room. The women huddled in a corner, whispering. Uncle Angelo and Poppa leaned over and listened. I kind of wondered what they were saying, but I was too busy having fun with my cousins running in and out of the clothes racks to pay much attention to them.

Then there he was!

Uncle Carmen came out of the dressing room wearing a beautiful navy blue suit, a crisp white shirt, and a smart black tie. I must say, he looked sharp.

Uncle stood up on a platform and viewed himself in a three-way mirror. He smiled a little smile at himself as we all crowded around him. Everyone told Uncle Carmen how distinguished and handsome he looked.

"Bello, bello, figlio mio!" said Nana with tears in her eyes.

Mr. Herbie started taking measurements. Uncle Carmen protested. "I'm just looking! This is quite a fine suit, but I'm not taking it today."

"Carmen!" exclaimed Nana. "You no hear the good news! When you were busy gettin' dressed, this nice man, he tell us you won a contest! You won a free suit!"

Wow! No one in my family had ever won a contest before!

"Contest?" said Mr. Herbie with his mouth open.

"YEAH! The CONTEST!" said Nana, staring straight at Mr. Herbie with a big smile.

"Oh, yes, yes . . . the contest!" Mr. Herbie stuttered.

"But this is a very expensive suit," said Uncle Carmen.

"You no worry about the price. You a contest winner! You a lucky man!" said Nana to a very puzzled-looking Uncle Carmen. "Now, you go change, Carmen. Go—go!"

Uncle went back to the dressing room. He paused at the doorway, turned his head, looked at us all, then disappeared through the curtains. Then something really weird happened! My entire family rushed to the cash register! "Uh, I think I got a twenty here," said Uncle Angelo.

"Let me look through my purse," said Aunt Pat.

Aunt Flo wrote a check, and Mom pulled out some singles.

"What about the contest?" I asked.

"Shhh! You say nothing! This is a family secret!" whispered Nana.

Uncle Carmen came out of the dressing room, and Aunt Pat grabbed his arm. "I brought a camera. Let's all go outside for a photograph!"

Everyone agreed. Mr. Herbie came out, too, and he took the picture. We all smiled for the camera, but no one smiled like Uncle Carmen. "I sure am a lucky guy!" he exclaimed with a tremendous grin and a wink to Nana. And Nana gave him a big smile right back!

Many things have happened since that day. Not everyone is still around, and those of us who are have grown and changed in different ways. Uncle Carmen is now the president of his own company.

But I will always remember the big day that my entire family went shopping for Uncle's new suit!

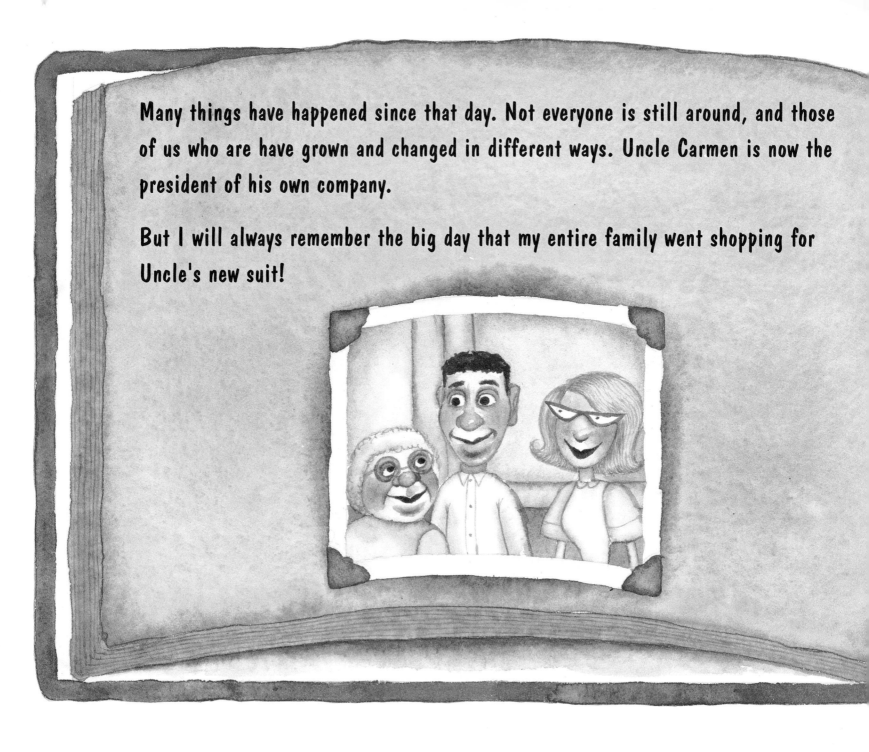

E   Passen, Lisa
Pa
        Uncle's new suit

          C 1